Arbor Day Tree

Written and Illustrated by Dee Smith

Copyright © 2018

Visit Deesignery.com

A celebration will soon be underway.

We celebrate trees on dear Arbor Day!

We celebrate the wondrous things they allow us to do.

We can make a big difference by just planting a few.

"Hello there," I say to my
Arbor Day Tree.

You are small now, but grand, one day, you shall be.

We celebrate trees because we know how important they are.

A tree in nature is a bright shining luminous star.

They help supply us with food, shelter, beauty and shade.

They create scenes that do not seem to dull, wither or fade.

Some are decked with Ivy. Some are speckled. Some are bare.

For each tree we celebrate. For each tree we care.

I take my Arbor Day Tree to my favorite spot.

I slowly unload my small tree
from its small orange pot.

I pat the last of the soil that surrounds my small Arbor Day Tree.

What a celebration!

What a lovely sight to see!

Happy Arbor Day!

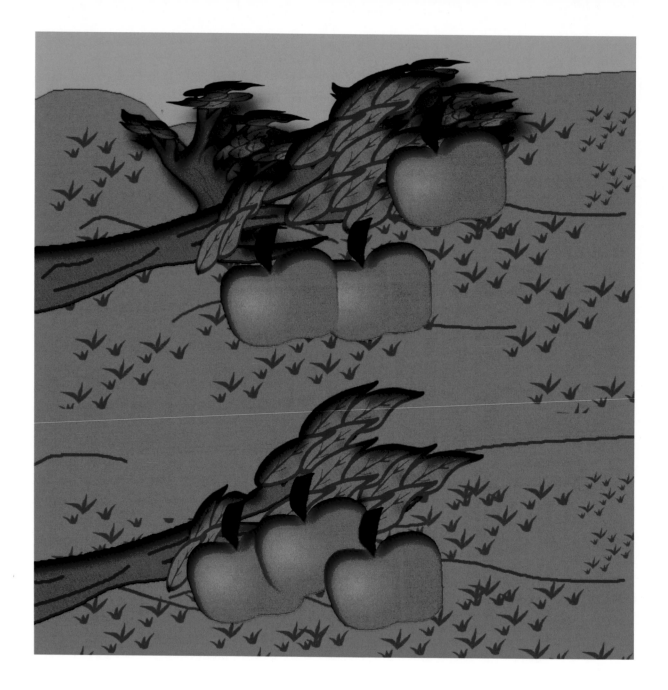

SURPRISE!

Bonus Cut and Color Simple
Arbor Day Craft

From the Author as a special thanks for reading this book!

Enjoy!

Arbor Day- Stand Up Tree

Materials: Scissors, tape, crayons

Instructions:

- **Make a copy of the following image.**
- **Color your tree and stand (the bar below).**
- **Loosely cut out the tree and bar below it.**
- **Tape ends together.**
- **Create a stand up tree craft!**

Thank You!

Thank you so much for reading this book.
It means the world to me!
If you liked the book I would much appreciate if you would write a Review on Amazon. I am so thankful for each and every person supporting my dream of being a writer for children. Because you have read this book, yes that means YOU too! Thanks Again!
Stay tuned for more titles on my website Deesignery.com

Regards,
Dee

About the Author:

My name is Dee Smith. I am an Author and Illustrator. My hobbies include graphic design, puppetry, balloon twisting, drawing and of course writing. I am dedicated to my mission of keeping children entertained in fun and innovative ways.

See what the Buzz is all about!
Take a journey to Bee-ville

Read this fun series about a small bee that goes on big adventures and learns along the way!

Made in the USA
Columbia, SC
04 April 2019